First

Comes Spring

A N N E   R O C K W E L L

HarperCollinsPublishers

Library of Congress Cataloging-in-Publication Data
Rockwell, Anne F.
  First comes spring.

  Summary: Bear Child notices that the clothes he
wears, the things everyone does at work and play,
and other parts of his world all change with the seasons.
  1. Children's stories, American. [1. Seasons—
Fiction. 2. Change—Fiction 3. Bears—Fiction]
I. Title.
PZ7.R5943Fi 1985   [E]   84-45331
ISBN 0-694-00106-6
ISBN 0-690-04455-0 (lib. bdg.)
ISBN 0-06-107412-8 (pbk.)

First paperback edition, 1991.

For Hannah,
Elizabeth and Oliver

Wake up, Bear Child.
Look out your window.

The daffodils and tulips are up.
The apple tree has blossoms.

This is what Bear Child wears today—
rubber boots, overalls, a flannel shirt
and a Windbreaker jacket.

For spring has come to town.
Everyone is busy.

What are they doing?

They are working and playing.

swinging

putting up birdhouses

putting away winter clothes

coloring Easter Eggs

riding bicycles

jumping rope

having parades

making mud pies

fertilizing the lawn

watching the birds come back

washing windows

flying kites

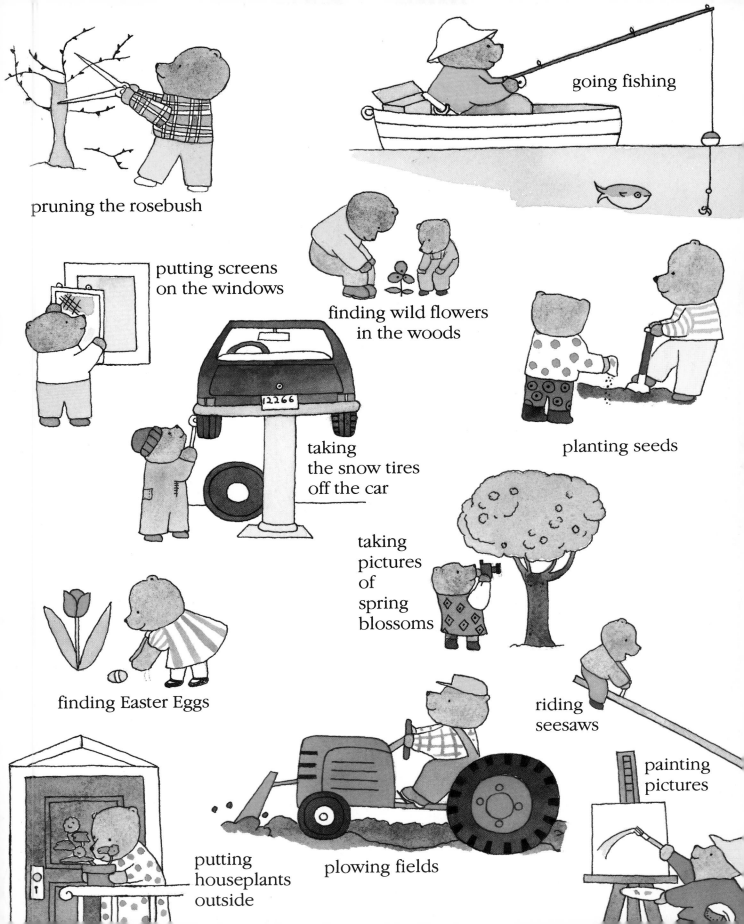

pruning the rosebush

going fishing

putting screens
on the windows

finding wild flowers
in the woods

planting seeds

taking
the snow tires
off the car

taking
pictures
of
spring
blossoms

finding Easter Eggs

riding
seesaws

painting
pictures

putting
houseplants
outside

plowing fields

The grass is green on the lawn.
The apple tree has little green apples.

Now this is what Bear Child wears—
sneakers, shorts and a T-shirt.

For summer has come to town.
Everyone is busy.

What are they doing?

They are working and playing.

watching ants

swimming

buying ice cream

reading in a hammock

weeding the garden

blowing soap bubbles

mowing the lawn

watering the rosebush

painting the house

selling lemonade

washing the car

drying clothes
in the sun

cooking
outdoors

eating
corn on the cob

playing in
the wading pool

camping out

playing
baseball

building
a new house

sailing

The apples are red.
Orange and yellow leaves fall to the ground.

Now this is what Bear Child wears—
new shoes, corduroy pants, a sweater
and a book bag.

For fall has come to town.
Everyone is busy.

What are they doing?

They are working
and playing.

picking
apples

watching
the birds
fly
south

canoeing

going
to school

raking
leaves

building
towers of blocks

gathering
nuts

playing football

feeding
the birds

dressing up
for Halloween

carving
a jack-o'-lantern

moving into
the
new house

picking
pumpkins

chopping
wood

cutting
down
the flower stalks

putting up
storm
windows

putting
the houseplants
indoors

making apple pie

buying
new clothes

putting
snow tires
on
the car

The trees have lost their leaves.
Snowflakes cover the ground.

Now this is what Bear Child wears—
rubber boots, a snowsuit, a scarf,
a cap and warm mittens.

For winter has come to town.
Everyone is busy.

What are they doing?

They are working
and playing.

ice-skating

visiting
Santa Claus

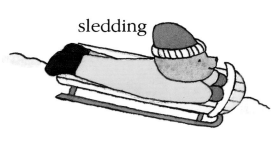

sledding

having colds

buying
presents

lighting
Hanukkah
candles

singing carols

making
angels

drinking cocoa

wrapping presents

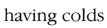

plowing the street

putting
a
wreath
on
the door

putting
suet balls
out for
the birds

bringing
a Christmas tree
home

shoveling
the walk

throwing
snowballs

building
an igloo

skiing

putting
lights
on
the
Christmas
tree

baking cookies

The Bear Family sits
by the nice, warm fire.